# The Chimp King

Written by
Hannah Welchman

Illustrated by
Peter Levy

The chimp king swings in the treetops.

He grips the trees as he swings. He jumps from tree to tree, twisting and turning in the air.

He is quick, and as strong as an ox.

The chimp king jumps onto the treetop platform.

Crowds of chimps start to yell and clap.

The chimp king stands up high and sniffs the air.

A gust of wind brings the smell of rain.
Then it starts to rain.

The raindrops hit the chimp king
with hard thuds.

This chimp is the seventh chimpanzee to be king.

But a champ is not a champ for long.

The chimp king must win all the tests to keep the crown.

Tonight the tests finish. Tonight it ends.

Can the chimp king keep the crown?

The crowd is still.

"This is the test," growls a chimpanzee from the crowd.
"A monster with big ears took the chimp flag. We need it back.
You must get the flag from the top of the high hill in the west."

"You must bring the flag back to us. Then you can keep the crown," growls the chimp in the crowd.

The chimp king stands still.
Then he swings off into the trees.

In the rainstorm, the chimp king looks to the west. He can see the high hill.

The trail up the hill is steep.
The air is thick and the rocks are sharp.

The mud on the tracks sucks him in.

At midnight, the chimp king stands
at the top of the hill.
He sees a dark hut.

A monster with big ears stands in the
starlight.

The chimp king thumps his chest.
He runs and he jumps.
He jumps high into the air.

He bumps into the monster
and lands at the hut with a crash.

The chimp grabs the flag.

Quick as a flash,
he runs back down the hill.

At the treetop platform, the crowd of chimps waits for him.

The chimp king swings up to the top of the trees.

The crowd starts to yell and stamp.
The yells are sharp and clear in the night.

The chimp king lands on the platform.
He grips the flag and lifts it high.

"Chimpanzees, I am still the king!
I will keep my crown!"